FOR JOAN, WHO IS NOT EASILY FOOLED
—S.K.

TO MY FRIEND ÉLISABETH AND LITTLE SOPHIE
—J.B.

Text copyright © 2011 by Stephen Krensky
Illustrations copyright © 2011 by Josée Bisaillon

Carolrhoda Books
A division of Lerner Publishing Group, Inc.
241 First Avenue North
Minneapolis, MN 55401 U.S.A.

Website address: www.lernerbooks.com

Library of Congress Cataloging-in-Publication Data

Krensky, Stephen.
    The great moon hoax / by Stephen Krensky ; illustrations by Josée Bisaillon.
       p.   cm.
    Summary: Two newsboys in 1830s New York sell copies of the New York Sun reporting that a
powerful telescope has found exotic animals and structures on the moon. Based on a true story.
    ISBN: 978–0–7613–5110–8 (lib. bdg. : alk. paper)
    [1. Newspaper vendors—Fiction. 2. Newspapers—Fiction. 3. Hoaxes—Fiction. 4. New York (N.Y.)—
History—1775–1865—Fiction.] I. Bisaillon, Josée, ill. II. Title.
PZ7.K883Gr 2011
[Fic]—dc22   2009026782

Manufactured in the United States of America
1 – DP – 12/31/10

THE GREAT MOON HOAX

Stephen Krensky

ILLUSTRATIONS BY
Josée Bisaillon

CAROLRHODA BOOKS
Minneapolis

"HEY, JAKE! WE'RE GOING TO BE LATE."

Twelve-year-old Jake Vernon opened his eyes.
He had been dreaming about breakfast in bed. This
surprised him since he rarely had time for breakfast
and even more rarely slept in a bed.

"I'm up, Charlie, I'm up," said Jake, jumping to his
feet. Both he and Charlie were newsboys for the *New
York Sun*. They had no homes or families of their
own, and where they spent the night depended on
how many pennies they had in their pockets.

Monday's sales had been a bit slow.
So they had slept for free on crates in a
dark alley. Now it was almost dawn.

The city's new gas lamps glowed softly
over the cobblestones as Jake and Charlie
made their way to the *Sun*'s office. At that
hour the streets were free of the horse-drawn
wagons that would clog them later in the day.
As always in August, though, the smell of
garbage filled the heavy air.

Ten boys were already in line when Jake and Charlie arrived. Each would pay sixty-seven cents for every hundred copies of the *Sun* they bought. The newspapers sold for a penny each, so a newsboy could make a profit of thirty-three cents on each hundred. But if he wasn't careful, he could lose money because unsold papers could not be returned.

The more experienced boys checked the Tuesday headlines before deciding how many papers to buy.

"There's a murder," said Jake.

"Just one?" Charlie didn't read as well as Jake, but he prided himself on a good pair of lungs. "Any fires?"

"Never mind the fires. Listen to this . . . A scientist named Sir John Herschel has made *'great astronomical discoveries'* in South Africa."

"Astronomical?" Charlie repeated.

"In the night sky," Jake explained.

"And where's South Africa?" Charlie asked.

"Far away," said Jake.

"Farther than Jersey?"

Jake nodded.

THE SUN.

ASTRONOMICAL DISCOVERIES

In fact, South Africa was eight thousand miles from New York. But this was just the kind of news the *Sun* relished. Founded two years earlier in 1833, its four pages were full of personal and unusual stories. And if those stories were shocking, so much the better.

After buying their papers, the boys hit the streets.

"NEW TELESCOPE SEES ALL!" Jake shouted from his usual corner.

"AMAZING SECRETS TO BE REVEALED!"

"EARTH IN DANGER" cried Charlie, who stretched the truth whenever possible.

Jake and Charlie sold out their papers before noon. They had time for a long nap before treating themselves to a fine oyster dinner.

"Here's to *astronomical discoveries*," said Charlie.

Jake nodded. "And the *Sun* says there's more to come. This is the beginning of a series." He looked out the window at the darkening sky. "If you had a telescope like that, what would you look at?"

"My brother lives in Boston," said Charlie.

"Maybe I'd have a look at him."

"I don't think telescopes work that way," said Jake.
"Well, they should," Charlie insisted, which to his mind settled the matter.

On Wednesday, the second article appeared. It described animals on the moon's surface. There were herds of brown quadrupeds, like small bison, but with a hairy veil that crossed "the whole breadth of the forehead and united to the ears."

There was also a creature "of a bluish lead color, about the size of a goat, with a head and beard like him, and a single horn . . . it seemed an agile sprightly creature, running with great speed, and springing from the green turf with all the unaccountable antics of a young lamb or kitten."

Even more unusual was something spotted near an island, "a strange amphibious creature of a spherical form, which rolled with great velocity across the pebbly beach."

"HEAVENS FILLED
WITH BUFFALO!"

"MOON BOWLED OVER
BY SEA MONSTER!"

"Astonishing!" said passengers boarding the trains at Union Square.

"Charming," said the ladies sipping tea at Delmonico's Café a few blocks away, while still wondering if such animals were dangerous.

But everyone was curious. The moon had always seemed so distant, so dull. Now things had changed. What would the *Sun* report next?

"VOLCANOES BLOW tOPS IN MOONLIGHT!"
"BEAVERS WATCHING US FROM ABOVE!"

Jake and Charlie did not have to say more than that. Thursday's paper described the moon's physical landscape. Vast oceans bordered "circular or oval mountainous ridges," many "in full volcanic eruption." There were many yellowish white craters as well, the largest of which was called the "Lake of Death."

More surprising, though, was the moon beaver. It looked much like the beavers on Earth—the kind that furriers liked to turn into hats—except for one thing. The moon beaver walked upright on two legs. As if that wasn't enough, it "carries its young in its arms like a human being, and moves with an easy gliding motion. Its huts are constructed better and higher than those of many tribes of human savages, and from the appearance of smoke in nearly all of them, there is no doubt of its being acquainted with the use of fire."

Jake and Charlie sold every
paper they could get their hands
on. And they could have sold even
more. They felt as rich as the
businessman John Jacob Astor.

That night they took a room at a boardinghouse.

"Well, do you think those moon animals would ever come here?" Jake wondered.

"Beavers don't fly," Charlie pointed out.

"Do you think we could ever go there?"

"We don't fly, either," Charlie reminded him. He jingled the coins in his pocket. "Anyway, we ate proper again tonight, and now we're sleeping in a bed. With a mattress and clean sheets."

"But it might be possible," said Jake. "Imagine visiting another world. That would be a trip to remember."

"WE ARE NOT ALONE!"

Friday's installment began with more details about great red hills and craggy cliffs. But then it took a new direction. Unexpectedly, "four successive flocks of large winged creatures" appeared. "They averaged four feet in height, were covered, except on the face, with short and glossy copper-colored hair, and had wings composed of a thin membrane, without hair, lying snugly upon their backs from the top of the shoulders to the calves of their legs."

The telescope's gaze followed
these seemingly peaceful creatures
into the water. There they swam
in comfort, occasionally unfurling
their wings to shake out the water.

Later, Jake actually read the whole article aloud to Charlie.

"So what if the man-bats flew down here?" Jake asked when he was done.

"I'd be very happy," said Charlie.

"Because you'd want to meet them?"

"No, because we'd sell more papers than even I can carry." He sighed. "But they won't come."

"Why not?"

"They won't leave their temple with the gold roof you told me about. The one with the giant pillars seventy feet high. They probably have to guard it day and night." Charlie whistled. "I'll bet it's worth a pretty penny."

Another valuable structure was revealed the next day. It was "an equitriangular temple, built of polished sapphire, or of some resplendent blue stone." This stone reflected the twinkling light of the sun and reflected it back in a thousand golden points.

"I can see the treasure hunters lining up now," said Jake. "If only there was a moon ship to take them aloft."

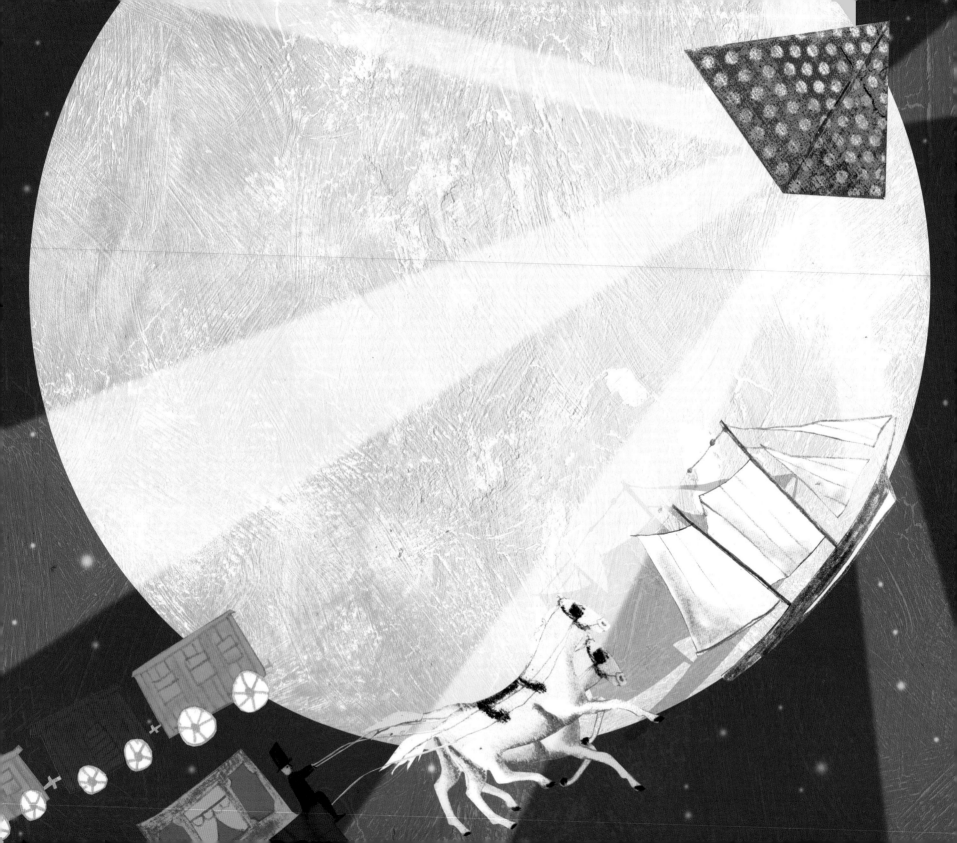

Two more reports followed, though with no stunning new revelations. And then the series ended. Apparently, the wondrous new telescope had been damaged in a fire. Nobody seemed to know when it would be working again.

"Too bad," said Charlie, patting his stomach. "I could get used to this."

"I wonder what will happen tomorrow," said Jake.

Charlie nodded. "Maybe somebody will start a war," he said.

But nobody did.

A few weeks later, there was news of a different kind. The moon stories were a hoax! They were a ruse, a trick. Or at least that's what everyone claimed. And the *Sun* wasn't denying it. The paper was too busy counting all the money it had been making lately.

That night Jake and Charlie lay against a brick wall, trying to make themselves comfortable.

"Are you disappointed all that moon stuff wasn't true?" Charlie asked.

Jake looked up at the stars. "No, not really. It was fun to think about, and I can still do that. It's really all about the words. Even if they're not quite true, they can make us see amazing things. Someday maybe I'll write my own stories, and when I do . . ."

"I'll shout it from the rooftops!" said Charlie.

And with that promise shared between them, they both fell fast asleep.

In 1833, when the *New York Sun* began publishing, most city newspapers were largely bought by subscription and delivered to established businesses or the homes of wealthy people. But Benjamin Day, publisher of the *Sun*, hoped to reach a wider audience, readers who would buy the paper on their way to work or when traveling through town. So he employed newsboys to sell his newspaper in the streets. (The first one hired was Bernard Flaherty, a ten-year-old who answered Day's advertisement for "men" to sell newspapers.)

Of course, it helped sales if the boys had some shocking news to shout headlines about. And in the summer of 1835, spectacular and outrageous reports of images from the moon fit the *Sun*'s needs perfectly.

Although some people were skeptical from the beginning, it was only a few weeks after the series stopped that news of the hoax surfaced. It wasn't that Sir John Herschel didn't exist. He did. It wasn't that he wasn't a famous astronomer. He was. But when he was finally tracked down in South Africa (where he did indeed live), he knew nothing about a new, more powerful telescope and he had made no new discoveries about the moon.

All that had been made up. The *Sun* never officially admitted to anything, and its editor, Richard Adams Locke, never stated that he had written the articles himself. But it was widely assumed that he was the author. The moon series made a lasting mark on the *Sun*, which burned brightly for over a hundred years before it finally ceased publication in 1950.